Jewel

The sparkly mist cleared away, leaving Sophie and Jewel standing alone in the darkness at a crossroads on a grassy heath. Sophie looked around, feeling utterly bewildered. A minute ago she'd been at a noisy, colourful fairground – and now she was in the middle of nowhere, in the middle of the night! She patted Jewel's wooden neck for comfort.

To her amazement, he snorted and shook his head. Jewel wasn't wooden at all! He was a real pony. Sophie stroked his thick, warm mane, and he reached his head round to nuzzle at her hand.

"What's going on?" Sophie breathed. "Where *are* we?"

Also available
Sparkle
Brightheart
Star

Look out for
Crystal
Flame

Magic Pony Carousel

Jewel

MACMILLAN CHILDREN'S BOOKS

A Working Partners Book

With special thanks to Holly Skeet

First published 2006 by Macmillan Children's Books
a division of Macmillan Publishers Limited
20 New Wharf Road, London N1 9RR
Basingstoke and Oxford
www.panmacmillan.com

Associated companies throughout the world

ISBN-13: 978-0-330-44044-8
ISBN-10: 0-330-44044-6

1 3 5 7 9 8 6 4 2

A CIP catalogue record for this book is available
from the British Library.

Printed and bound in Great Britain by Mackays of Chatham plc, Kent

Contents

1. Sophie's Adventure Begins

"Got it!" Sophie waved her long bamboo pole. It had a yellow plastic duck swinging madly on the hook at the end.

"Well done!" said her mum.

Sophie's dad unhooked the duck and handed it to the woman standing on the other side of the inflatable pool. Lots of bright yellow ducks bobbed on the water, waiting to be hooked. The woman smiled at Sophie and told her to choose a prize.

Sophie picked a key ring in the shape of a pretty jet-black pony wearing a jewelled browband. She loved ponies more than anything else in the world! "Thank you!" she said to the woman running the stall.

Beside her there was a crash, as Sophie's little sister Molly threw down her bamboo pole. "This is a stupid game!" Molly grumbled. "I can't hook any of the ducks. They keep swimming away!"

Sophie sighed. Molly was only four, and she got very cross when she couldn't do everything Sophie did.

"Let's go and find something else," said their dad. He took Sophie and Molly by the hand and they wandered further into the fair. It was very busy, and Sophie held on tightly to her dad's hand. She put her other hand into her pocket to check her pony key ring hadn't fallen out. The little jet-black pony felt warm and smooth underneath her fingers.

There were rides and stalls *everywhere*! Sophie thought she'd never be able to decide what to go on next. Her mum pointed to a stall where you had to kick a football into a goal to win prizes. But Sophie didn't think she could win a better prize than her pony key ring, so she shook her head.

Just then, she spotted a pointy golden roof peeping out from behind the football game. Tugging her dad's hand, she led him over.

"Look!" Sophie cried. "It's a pony carousel!" It was the prettiest fairground ride she had ever seen. The wooden ponies were really lifelike, their eyes twinkling and their tails floating out behind them.

"Would you like to have a turn?" asked Sophie's mum.

"Yes please!" Sophie said. There was nothing she wanted more than to ride round on the carousel, holding one of the twisty golden poles.

But Molly had spotted something else. "I want to go on the giant teacups!" she said, pointing.

Sophie stared at her sister in surprise. How could giant spinning teacups be better than the beautiful pony carousel? Molly started to drag their dad towards the teacups. Sophie felt a bit cross. Now she wouldn't be able to go on the carousel!

Her mum bent down and gave her

shoulders a squeeze. "Shall we stay here while your dad takes Molly on the teacups?" she said. Sophie nodded eagerly.

She walked to the bottom of the steps leading up to the carousel. There were so many ponies! There was a stocky toffee-coloured pony with a stiff mane and bells and ribbons on his harness – the kind of pony Sophie had seen pulling sleighs in pictures. And a handsome bay pony with brave brown eyes and a tail that flowed all the way down to the floor. He had an old-fashioned saddle as though he was a medieval knight's pony.

Then Sophie gasped out loud. One of the ponies looked exactly like her key ring! He was jet black – the colour of a dark, velvety night – and across his forehead was a brow-band decorated with sparkling pink and violet jewels. When Sophie peered closer, she saw a little name-scroll hanging from the golden pole on his back. It read, *Jewel*! It was the perfect name for such a beautiful pony.

Someone coughed politely close by, making Sophie jump. A tall gentleman was standing behind her. He was grandly dressed in a red velvet suit and a red and green striped top hat. He bowed to Sophie, sweeping the hat from his head.

"Welcome to Barker's Magic Pony Carousel!" he declared. His blue eyes twinkled. "My name is Mr Barker."

Sophie stared at him. "Did you just say *Magic* Pony Carousel?" she said.

Mr Barker grinned. "Oh yes! Most definitely magic. Would you like a ride on the carousel?"

"Oh yes, please!" Sophie gasped.

"Well, I have just a few tickets left for the next ride," he said. He reached into his pocket and took out some tiny pieces of pink paper. "The name of your pony is written on the ticket you choose. Think hard about which pony you'd like it to be!" Mr Barker held out the tickets to Sophie, along with a magnifying glass. "Pick one! And have a look at it with the magnifying glass. The writing can be a little hard to read sometimes," he explained.

Sophie thought hard about the midnight-black pony that looked like the one on her key ring. Then with trembling fingers she chose one of the little pink tickets. She lifted the magnifying glass and peered at the tiny piece of paper. The swirly writing *was* hard to read – but it definitely said Jewel.

"It's Jewel!" she told him excitedly.

"Ah! That's a very special pony." Mr Barker beamed. "Now, quickly, on you get, we're ready to start. Climb aboard, everyone! All aboard the Magic Pony Carousel!"

Sophie ran up the steps and weaved her way through the other wooden ponies until she reached Jewel. "I'm so glad your name was on my ticket!" she whispered, stroking his forehead. The painted wood felt silky under her fingers. Jewel's dark eyes seemed to look straight into hers as though he was glad too. Sophie gave him a quick kiss on the nose, then climbed into the saddle.

Mr Barker checked that everyone was on their pony before he twirled a big golden handle to start the carousel. There was a grating noise, then music rang out and Sophie felt Jewel soar into the air as the carousel moved off. She gripped the golden pole tightly and waved to her mum as she whirled past her. The fairground slipped by in a blur of silvery lilac light, the tinkling music filled Sophie's ears and the crowds seemed to fade away.

Sophie blinked. The other children on their wooden ponies had vanished too, and she and Jewel were galloping through swirls of sparkling mist. The sunlight dimmed until they were surrounded by heavy black shadows . . .

Suddenly Sophie knew they weren't in the fairground any more!

2. A Shady Business

The sparkly mist cleared away, leaving Sophie and Jewel standing alone in the darkness at a crossroads on a grassy heath. There was just one house in the distance, with a dim light burning in the window. From somewhere far away, Sophie could hear a church clock striking – ten, eleven, twelve strokes. It was midnight! Sophie looked around, feeling utterly bewildered. A minute ago she'd been at a noisy, colourful fairground – and now she was in the middle of nowhere, in the middle of the night! She patted Jewel's wooden neck for comfort.

To her amazement, he snorted and shook his head. Jewel wasn't wooden at all! He was a real pony. Sophie stroked his thick, warm mane, and he reached his head round to nuzzle at her hand. The jewels in his browband caught the moonlight and glittered brightly.

"What's going on?" Sophie breathed. "Where *are* we?"

As her eyes got used to the darkness, she realized she was no longer wearing her favourite jeans with the sequinned butterflies, or her pink T-shirt. Instead, she was dressed in shiny black satin breeches, soft leather riding boots and a white shirt with ruffles on the collar and cuffs. Hanging from her shoulders was a magnificent black velvet cloak lined with purple silk. Sophie wriggled her feet in the close-fitting boots. She felt dressed for adventure!

A flash of white among the trees by the road caught her eye, and she walked Jewel over to see what it was. Jewel didn't seem very happy about walking anywhere. Sophie could feel him trembling beneath her, and his bit jangled as he nervously tossed his head. "Hey, boy," Sophie murmured, patting his neck again. "It's OK, we're just going to see what that is." Sophie had ridden nervous ponies before, and she knew she had to take everything very slowly and not force Jewel on when he was frightened.

The flash of white turned out to be a poster nailed to the tree. Sophie edged Jewel really close so she could read it. Maybe it would help her work out where she was.

WANTED
HAVE YOU SEEN THIS MAN?

Sophie gasped. It was a "Wanted" poster! Sophie eased it off its nail so she could read it better in the moonlight. Below the heavy black letters was a drawing of a scary-looking man, with thick black eyebrows and an ugly scar down the side of his face.

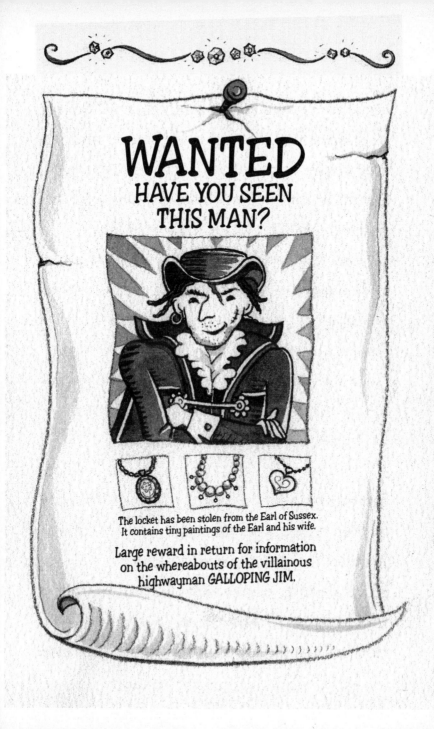

Next to his picture were some drawings of jewellery, including a beautiful golden locket with a pattern of roses on it. More writing explained that the locket had been stolen from the Earl of Sussex. It contained tiny paintings of the Earl and his wife.

At the very bottom of the poster was a message:

Large reward in return for information on the whereabouts of the villainous highwayman GALLOPING JIM.

Sophie shuddered. "I wouldn't like to meet Galloping Jim tonight," she said out loud, hooking the poster back on its nail.

"Me neither," someone replied.

Sophie nearly jumped out of the saddle in shock. Who said that? She looked round, thinking someone must have crept up behind them, but she was still on her own.

On her own, that is, except for Jewel.

Sophie frowned. Then she leaned forward and whispered in Jewel's ear, "Was that you?"

Jewel nodded.

Sophie sat back up quickly. "But ponies can't talk! What's happening?"

Jewel tossed his mane. "Didn't Mr Barker tell you it was a Magic Pony Carousel?" he said. "All ponies can talk, but most people don't know how to listen. The carousel's magic ticket means you can understand me. Anyone else would just think I was whinny-ing."

Sophie felt a bubble of excitement growing inside her. "I knew there was something special about that pony carousel!" she said.

"The carousel has brought us here to help someone," Jewel explained. "But don't worry, the magic will take us back before your mum notices you've gone."

"Who are we meant to help?" Sophie looked around. "There's no one else here!"

Jewel snorted. "I'm not sure exactly. But we'll know when we find the right person. I just wish it wasn't so dark," he muttered. "Why do we have to have an adventure in the middle of the night?"

"Don't be scared, Jewel," said Sophie. She reached forward and rubbed the soft bit of hair behind his ears.

Jewel stretched out his neck. "Ooh, that feels nice. A little higher . . . Wait! What's that?"

A rattling, thudding noise was coming from further along the road. Sophie held the reins tightly to stop Jewel from running away.

The noise grew louder and louder until an old-fashioned coach burst out of the shadows, pulled by four magnificent grey horses. Their harnesses jingled and their tails streamed out behind them as they galloped along.

"We'd better get out of the way," Jewel said nervously, and he stepped into the shadow of the trees.

The coach was going so fast that the candle lanterns hanging on each corner swung wildly from side to side. Peering forward, Sophie could see the passengers inside hanging on for dear life. The coach didn't look a comfy ride on such a stony, rutted track.

As the coach drew level with Sophie and

Jewel, a chestnut pony shot out from behind some trees on the other side of the road. A girl the same age as Sophie was urging the pony on as fast as she could.

Sophie stared at her in surprise. "She came out of nowhere!" she said to Jewel. "Do you think she wants to get on the coach?"

"I don't think so!" Jewel hissed back. "Watch!"

"Stand and deliver!" the girl called faintly, and her pony reared and neighed.

But the driver was going too fast to notice the girl and the pony lurking in the shadows. The coach just sped on, its wooden wheels bouncing over the stones.

As the coach and its passengers rattled safely away, Sophie got a chance to look at the girl properly. She looked almost ghostly in the moonlight, with her pale face and mass of white-blonde curls. She had a dark three-pointed hat pulled down over her forehead, and she was wearing a flowing cloak, simi-lar to Sophie's – and as she turned her pony, Sophie spotted a black satin mask across her eyes.

It was a highwaygirl!

3. Stand and Deliver!

Sophie had read about highwaymen in her favourite book of horse stories, but she'd never heard of a girl being one!

Suddenly an owl hooted and Jewel leaped sideways in surprise. Sophie tried to keep him still, but it was too late. His hoofs clattered on the stony ground, and the highwaygirl looked round sharply.

"Who's there?" she called.

Sophie gasped. "Jewel, what should we do?" she whispered.

"I don't think we can run away," he

whispered back. "She knows we're here now." With a snort, he stepped out of the shadows. Sophie felt very proud of him for being so brave.

The highwaygirl rode over to them. "Who are you?" she demanded.

"Please don't shoot us!" Sophie stammered.

Suddenly, to Sophie's astonishment, the girl laughed. "I'm not going to hurt you. I missed the coach again, didn't I?" she said.

Sophie nodded, still too startled to speak.

The girl grinned. "Never mind! I was watching an owl in the wood, and I lost track of time. Not that I wanted to stop the coach anyway. They'll all get home safe, with their money and jewels."

Sophie felt very confused. "You didn't want to stop the coach?"

The girl sighed. "I was supposed to stop it and steal the passengers' money. But I'm no good at it. I must be the worst highwaygirl ever." She smiled at Sophie. "I'm Lucy, by the way. What's your name?"

"I'm Sophie, and this is Jewel."

"Hello, Jewel." Lucy leaned forward to stroke Jewel's forehead. Suddenly she stopped and looked anxious. "You won't report me, will you, Sophie? If you went to the parish constable, I would get into terrible trouble."

Sophie guessed that the parish constable was a bit like the police. Her grandad was a policeman. He had told her that, when the police force had been formed almost two hundred years ago, highwaymen had caused them a lot of trouble. She and Jewel must have travelled back in time over two hundred years!

Lucy was still looking very worried. Sophie shook her head. "Don't worry, I won't say anything. Besides, I don't think you can get into much trouble for *not* stopping a coach!"

Lucy grinned again, her teeth flashing white in the shadows. "I suppose not. I'd better get home now. Where do you live?"

"Not around here," Sophie admitted. It was chilly, and the dark heath was a bit spooky for camping out. Jewel stamped his hoof, as though he didn't fancy a night outside either.

Lucy looked at her hopefully. "Well, why don't you come and stay at my uncle's house?"

Sophie hesitated. She ran her fingers

25

through Jewel's mane, trying to think. Could she trust Lucy? She seemed nice, but she dressed like a highwaygirl, even if she didn't really want to rob coaches.

"Please come!" said Lucy. "My uncle will be out playing cards, and there isn't anyone else to keep me company. It would be so nice to have someone to talk to."

Sophie was very tempted, but she needed to ask Jewel first. "Hold on a minute – I, er, I need to check Jewel's girth," she said. "His saddle feels a bit loose." She wheeled Jewel round. They walked a little way and Sophie dismounted so she could talk to Jewel while she pretended to tighten his girth.

"What do you think, Jewel? Lucy seems really nice, and we don't have anywhere else to stay."

Jewel nodded. "You're right. I hope there's

a nice warm stable for me! And maybe when we get to Lucy's house, we'll find whoever it is we need to help."

Sophie led him back to where Lucy was waiting. "We'd love to stay with you, thank you," she said.

Lucy jumped off her pony and gave Sophie a hug. "Oh, I'm so glad! You can share my room, and Jewel can go in the stable with Brown Bess." She stroked her pony's mane, and Brown Bess snorted happily. She was a big chestnut pony, with a pretty, intelligent face. She seemed friendly too, stretching her nose forward to nuzzle Jewel.

The girls climbed back on to their ponies and Lucy led the way, deeper into the trees. Jewel shivered as the shadows swallowed them up.

Sophie patted his neck. "Not long now, Jewel."

After a while, Lucy slowed down and twisted round in the saddle to look at Sophie. "We're nearly there, but the path's really narrow and there are lots of brambles, so watch out."

Sophie could hardly see the path at all! She had to concentrate very hard to steer Jewel between the prickly bushes. Sophie was peering so carefully at the path that it was a shock when Lucy said, "Here we are."

Sophie looked up and caught her breath. They were standing in front of the most rickety, tumbledown house she had ever seen!

4. Lonely Lucy

The house looked as if no one had lived there for a very long time. Brambles sprawled over the fence into the garden. The red-tiled roof was full of holes, and several of the windows were broken. The green paint on the front door was peeling away in long curls. Sophie began to think that she wasn't going to get a very comfy night's sleep.

"The stable's this way," said Lucy, leading them round the side of the house. The stables badly needed a coat of paint, but at least the stalls were dry, and fresh straw lay thickly on the floor.

"Will you be all right here?" Sophie whispered as she took off Jewel's saddle and bridle.

Jewel looked around. He swished his tail happily when he spotted a rack full of sweet-smelling hay. "Yum!" he said. "Don't worry about me, I'll be fine." He walked over and started munching a mouthful of hay.

Sophie felt very relieved. She put a snug-looking rug on Jewel, checked he had plenty of water, and then gave him one last hug before leaving the stable.

She followed Lucy to the front door and waited while she took a heavy iron key from underneath a large round stone by the doorstep. Staring up at the cracked windows, Sophie couldn't help wondering if she would have been more comfortable staying with Jewel in the stable.

As Lucy pushed open the door, Sophie let out a gasp.

"Looks different in here, doesn't it?" said Lucy.

Inside, the tumbledown house was more like a palace! Sophie stepped through the doorway and stared around. Her feet sank into a rich red carpet, and the walls were covered in gorgeous red and gold striped silk. A chandelier hung from the ceiling, the small glass drops twinkling in the candle-light.

"This is amazing!" Sophie said. She wished Jewel could see this too.

She walked into a room leading off the hallway and went over to stroke the soft velvet curtains that hung all the way down to the floor. She noticed a carved wooden box on a pretty table with spindly legs. The box was overflowing with beautiful jewellery, from

33

brooches and rings studded with glowing jewels to a long pearl necklace that spilt over the edge of the table like a silvery snake.

Sophie turned to Lucy, who was watching her from the doorway. "The house is so beautiful! But why is it falling down on the outside?"

"My uncle keeps the outside of the house looking ruined so people think there's no one living here," Lucy explained. "He doesn't like visitors." Before she could say anything else, a little silver clock standing next to the jewellery box began to chime one. "We'd better go to bed," said Lucy. "I have to get up early to make my uncle's breakfast."

She led Sophie up the stairs to a pretty bedroom with pale blue walls the exact colour of the summer sky. Two beds stood side by side under the window, draped in matching blue and silver eiderdowns.

"I wish my bedroom was like this," said Sophie. "It would be so cool to have two beds. I'd have friends to stay all the time!"

Lucy was taking a nightgown out of a drawer. She stopped and looked at Sophie, biting her lip. "Actually, no one has ever slept in that other bed," she confessed. "My uncle doesn't like me having any friends." She handed Sophie the nightgown and smiled. "I'm really glad I met you."

Sophie felt sorry for her new friend. "Isn't there anyone you can play with?" she asked, as she got changed into the pretty embroidered nightgown. It was very different from her pink and white spotty pyjamas at home.

Lucy jumped into her bed and pulled the sky-blue and silver cover round her knees. "There are some children in the village who I'd like to be friends with, but my Uncle Jim would never let me play with them."

Sophie frowned. "Why not?"

Lucy looked down at her knees and fiddled with a loose thread on the eider-down. Sophie guessed Lucy didn't like talking about her uncle, so she didn't ask any more questions. She snuggled into her cosy bed and put her head on the big fluffy pillow. This was the most exciting adventure she'd ever had!

Sophie woke to find sunlight streaming in through the curtains. Lucy was still curled up in bed, fast asleep. Downstairs, someone was shouting crossly. Sophie slipped out of bed and tiptoed along the landing. Peering over the banister, she caught sight of a tall, broad-shouldered man striding down the hall.

"Where's my breakfast, Lucy?" he yelled.

Sophie ducked back into the bedroom. She had a feeling Lucy's uncle wouldn't be too happy to have an unexpected guest.

Lucy was standing beside her bed, pulling on her clothes. "Sorry! Got to go!" she gasped to Sophie before she vanished out of the door, carrying her boots under her arm.

Sophie got dressed and crept down the stairs to the kitchen. Lucy was frying eggs in a big pan over a fire. Her uncle was nowhere to be seen.

"Can I help?" Sophie asked.

"Could you make some toast?" Lucy

pointed to some thick slices of bread on the table. "The toasting fork's over there."

Sophie gulped. She'd never tried to make toast by stabbing the bread on a big metal fork and holding it over a coal fire! The first slice fell into the flames, but Sophie quickly got the hang of it. Soon the kitchen was filled with the delicious smell of warm crispy bread. Sophie and Lucy loaded the breakfast on to a big gold tray and Lucy carefully carried it into the dining room.

Sophie peered around the door as Lucy

put the tray down in front of her uncle. As he glanced up to speak to Lucy, Sophie's heart jumped into her mouth. She had seen that face before!

Lucy's uncle was Galloping Jim, the famous highwayman!

5. Sophie in Shock

"Why didn't you tell me your uncle was Galloping Jim?" Sophie burst out as Lucy returned with the empty tray.

"You recognized him then?" Lucy said, looking very upset.

Sophie nodded. "I saw his face on a Wanted poster last night."

"I didn't want to scare you off," Lucy explained sadly. "I thought you might run away! I just wanted a friend, even if it was only for one night." To Sophie's dismay Lucy started to cry.

"Oh don't, please!" said Sophie, going over to give her a hug. She found a crisp white handkerchief in the pocket of her breeches and handed it to Lucy. "Is that why you have to be a highwaygirl?"

Lucy nodded.

"But why does your uncle want *you* to hold up coaches?" Sophie asked. "He's a highwayman himself!"

"He's too well known." Lucy blew her nose. "He can't risk being seen holding up a coach or Mr Joy the parish constable would catch him."

A shout from the dining room made them stop talking. Lucy darted off, wiping her eyes. Sophie followed her along the hall and peeked round the door.

"So, my girl, what did you get last night? A bag of gold coins? Some jewels? Hand it over!" Galloping Jim bellowed.

Lucy hung her head. "I didn't manage to stop the coach," she confessed.

"What, again?" roared her uncle. Sophie shuddered as Galloping Jim's eyebrows drew together in a fearsome frown. "You're worse than useless!" He banged his fist down on the table, making the plates jump. "It's no good. I'll have to go out myself tonight. I'm not letting you mess this one up, Lucy."

"Whose coach is it?" Lucy asked.

Galloping Jim spoke through a mouthful

of toast, spraying crumbs everywhere. "Lady Amelia Grey is off to a ball in her private coach. She'll be wearing all her best jewels! And I'll be waiting for her at the crossroads when her coach goes by." He sighed. "Really, if I have to hold up the coaches myself, I don't know why I bother letting you stay here. Go on, be off," he snarled. Lucy dodged as he threw a silver salt cellar after her.

Back in the kitchen, Sophie watched Lucy pace up and down angrily. "I can't let him hold up Lady Amelia's coach! But what can I do? If Uncle Jim gets any crosser with me, he'll send me to the poorhouse!" She swept her hand along the table, shoving the gold plates and engraved knives and forks to the floor with a crash. Then she sighed, got down on her knees and started to clear up.

"There must be something we can do," said Sophie as she bent down to help Lucy pick up the plates.

Lucy tried to smile. "Only the washing up," she said.

Sophie decided to talk to Jewel. She grabbed a couple of apples from the bowl on the table and dashed outside, telling Lucy she was going to feed the ponies.

Jewel was dozing in his stall next to Brown Bess. Sophie gently stroked him awake and broke the news.

"Galloping Jim is Lucy's uncle?" Jewel gasped.

"Yes, and he's going to hold up a coach tonight! Jewel, you know you said we were sent here to help someone? Well, I think we have to save Lucy from her uncle!"

Jewel nodded. "But how?" He thoughtfully chewed a mouthful of apple. "I know! Didn't Lucy mention a constable in the village?"

"That's right. His name is Mr Joy."

Jewel scraped his hoof on the floor. "We need to help him catch Galloping Jim tonight. But how can we make Mr Joy believe we're telling the truth? A house full of jewels in the middle of a forest sounds like something out of a fairy tale!" Suddenly his ears pricked up. "Do you remember that poster you saw on a tree?"

"Of course!" said Sophie. "That's how I recognized Galloping Jim."

"Ah, but what *else* was on it?" Jewel prompted.

Sophie pictured the poster in her head. "Well, there was a drawing of the locket that was stolen from the Earl of Sussex . . .

Jewel, you're a genius!" She threw her arms around his neck. "If I can find the locket in Galloping Jim's house, I can show it to Mr Joy. And I bet I know where it is. There's a jewellery box in the sitting room overflowing with necklaces and things. I'll go and look now."

"I'll wait here," Jewel called after her, "and then we can go and find Mr Joy."

Sophie ran back to the house. Lucy was still scrubbing pans in the kitchen.

"Don't worry! We've got a plan!" Sophie hissed as she sped past.

She tiptoed into the hallway. She couldn't risk making any noise in case Galloping Jim found her. As she tiptoed past the dining room she peeked round the door. He was drinking a cup of tea, scowling.

Sophie knew she had to be quick. She

crept into the sitting room and went over to the table. As she sorted through the jewellery, she noticed a beautiful chain like a fine silver rope. Could it be the locket? Suddenly she heard a chair scraping in the dining room. Galloping Jim was getting up! She pulled frantically at the chain — yes, this was it! On the end of the chain was a large silver oval, carved with delicate roses, that opened up to reveal two tiny portraits.

Sophie raced back to the kitchen, her heart thumping. "Lucy, I have to get to the village! Which way is it?"

Lucy looked alarmed. "You need to go back along the path and turn left by the big

oak tree. You're not going to tell the constable about Uncle Jim, are you? Sophie,
you mustn't!"

A tiny flicker of doubt went through
Sophie's mind. Were she and Jewel doing the
right thing? Lucy seemed so frightened. I
have to do this, she told herself firmly. Lucy
couldn't stay here with her wicked uncle
forever – she had to be rescued. This must be
what the carousel had sent her and Jewel
here for.

"Lucy, it will be all right. I promise it will.
Just trust me and Jewel. Meet us in the village this evening." Sophie shot out of the
back door, then popped her head back
round it. "And try not to worry!"

6. Jewel's Bright Idea

Sophie saddled up Jewel and rode back down the brambly path. She was a bit confused about which oak tree Lucy meant, but Jewel helped her out. He sniffed the air. "This way! I can smell smoke from the village chimneys."

They followed a twisty path through the woods. Not far from the edge of the forest there were some little white houses with thatched roofs.

Sophie heard a strange clinking sound. "What's that?" she said.

Jewel snorted. "It's the blacksmith's hammer," he explained. "We must be close to the forge."

They followed the noise to a long, low building. The door was open to reveal a fire burning brightly. A little boy with curly black hair was pumping a set of bellows to make the flames leap higher. Outside, a tall white-haired man with a bright red scarf round his neck was nailing a shoe to the hoof of a stocky brown and white horse. The blacksmith! He looked familiar, but Sophie couldn't work out why. She watched as he fixed the hot shoe in place.

It gave off a hiss of steam, but the horse stood very still.

A girl about the same age as Sophie came running round the corner. She stopped when she saw Sophie and smiled. "Hello!" she said. "Are you looking for someone?"

"Yes, I am," said Sophie. "I don't suppose you know where I'd find Mr Joy, do you? The parish constable?"

The girl laughed, her eyes sparkling. "You're in luck! That's his horse being shod, and he's the one holding the bridle." Then she ran off again, flashing another smile at Sophie.

The blacksmith carefully lowered the horse's hoof to the ground and straightened up, giving Sophie a friendly wink. She was sure she knew him! Of course – he looked just like Mr Barker from the carousel! But what would he be doing here?

The man holding the horse smiled at Sophie. "Did I hear you tell Ellen you wanted to talk to me?"

Sophie nodded. Her heart began to thud. She was going to tell Mr Joy about Galloping Jim, even though Lucy had begged her not to!

Mr Joy raised his eyebrows. "Why are you dressed up in your brother's clothes? Are you off on an adventure?"

Sophie blushed. She'd forgotten that girls would never wear trousers at this time. But the Magic Carousel obviously thought breeches and a ruffled shirt would be easier for riding through the forest. "Sort of. My name's Sophie. I have some information about Galloping Jim, the highwayman."

She pointed to another copy of the poster, which was nailed to the door of the forge.

The blacksmith whistled through his teeth, as though this was exciting news. The constable looked surprised and very serious. "Go on!"

"He's planning to rob Lady Amelia's coach tonight," Sophie explained in a rush. "If you hide in her coach you could catch him red-handed."

Sophie could see Mr Joy wasn't sure whether to believe her. She pulled the silver locket from under her cloak. "Look! This proves I'm not making it up."

"It's the Earl of Sussex's stolen locket!" Constable Joy turned it over in his hands, then looked up at Sophie. "You say Galloping Jim is planning another robbery tonight?"

"Yes! Lady Amelia is going to a ball, and he's going to wait for her coach at the cross-roads."

"Then this is our best chance to catch him!" said Mr Joy. "No one's ever been able to prove anything against that slippery rogue, but we might just do it! I'm sure Lady Amelia will help us."

Suddenly a small boy in a smart dark green suit ran up. "Message from the manor," he said to the blacksmith. "There was an accident yesterday and the coach-man has been hurt. He'll be all right in a few days," he added. "But one of Lady Amelia's carriage ponies put his hoof in a hole, hurting it badly and pulling off his shoe. Lady Amelia would like you to go and fit a new one. She won't be going to the ball tonight, not with one of her ponies lame and no coachman to drive her."

The blacksmith told the boy that he'd come to the manor later on. Mr Joy turned to Sophie. "That's a shame," he said. "We won't be able to catch Galloping Jim if there's no coach for him to rob!"

Sophie felt very disappointed. It had been such a good plan! She thanked Mr Joy anyway and trailed over to Jewel.

"What's the matter? Didn't he believe you?" asked Jewel when he saw Sophie looking miserable.

"Lady Amelia can't go to the ball!' Sophie explained. "One of her carriage ponies is lame. We'll have to think of something else."

Jewel didn't say anything for a few moments. Then he scraped the ground with his front hoof. "I could pull the coach,

55

Sophie. If the other pony is about the same size as me, the harness should fit."

Sophie threw her arms around his neck. "Jewel, that's so brave of you! I know you can do it. Come on, let's go and ask Mr Joy."

She led Jewel back over to the forge, where the blacksmith was finishing off the

last shoe. "Mr Joy, how big are Lady Amelia's carriage ponies?"

Mr Joy looked at Jewel. "Well, I'd say they're about the same size as your pony."

"Then Jewel can help pull the coach and we can catch Galloping Jim after all!"

Sophie declared. Suddenly she remembered that Mr Joy was the parish constable and she shouldn't be ordering him about. She felt her cheeks go bright red, but to her relief Mr Joy nodded.

"It's a good idea," he said. Then his face fell. "But we've still got no coachman."

Sophie stared at him in dismay. She'd forgotten that Lady Amelia's coach driver had been injured as well! Suddenly she saw the blacksmith looking at her intently, his eyes twinkling. He turned to Mr Joy.

"This girl could drive the coach, sir. After all – it is her pony!"

Sophie looked alarmed. "But I don't know how to!" she whispered to Jewel.

Jewel snorted. "I'll look after you. We can do it together. You just need to hold the reins and I'll tell you what to do. Ask him, go on."

Sophie took a deep breath. "Mr Joy? If Jewel takes the place of the lame pony, could I drive the coach?" She gazed pleadingly up at the constable.

Mr Joy was looking unsure about this. "Now, I don't know," he said. "There must be someone else we could ask."

Jewel whinnied, nudging the constable with his nose.

The blacksmith laughed and Mr Joy shook his head, smiling. "Anyone would think that pony understands exactly what we're saying!" he said. "Well, all right then. As long as I'm there to keep an eye on things, you should be safe. Let's go and see Lady Amelia right now and tell her she can go to the ball after all."

Sophie grinned and gave Jewel a big hug. They were going to catch Galloping Jim!

7. The Plot Thickens

Constable Joy mounted his sturdy brown and white horse, Henry. They led Sophie and Jewel straight to Grey Manor, Lady Amelia's enormous house.

Lady Amelia was in the stable-yard, stroking the lame pony. Lady Amelia was very beautiful, a bit younger than Sophie's mum, with curly brown hair piled high on her head. Her red silk dress was so long that it would have trailed on the ground if she hadn't had it looped up over one arm. Sophie could see that she was wearing delicate little red shoes with flowers embroidered on them, but she had wooden sandals strapped on underneath to keep them clean.

Next to Lady Amelia was an older lady, who had a very cross expression on her face. She was waving a fan and complaining loudly. "Amelia, dear, must we stay here much longer? The smell is simply dreadful, I feel quite ill," she grumbled.

But Lady Amelia was too worried about her lame pony to listen. "Poor Blackberry," she said, reaching over the stable door to rub the pony's nose. "He does look sorry for himself." She turned round and saw Sophie and Mr Joy leading Jewel and Henry across the cobbled yard. "Hello, Mr Joy. Have you heard about our accident?"

Mr Joy took off his hat and bowed. "Good day, My Lady. Actually, yes. I've come with a plan to help you go to the ball," he said.

"Really?" Lady Amelia looked interested. "Is this young lady going to help as well? It's so nice to see somebody in sensible clothes – this dress is completely unsuitable for the stable-yard." Lady Amelia beamed at Sophie, but the old lady looked horrified.

"Shocking!" she muttered. "A girl in breeches! Whatever next?"

"This is Sophie," said Mr Joy. "She's the one who's come up with the plan. My Lady, we think we can catch Galloping Jim. But we need your help too."

Lady Amelia clapped her hands. "How exciting!"

Mr Joy explained how Jewel was going to take the place of the lame pony and Sophie was going to drive the coach so they could catch Galloping Jim red-handed.

"What a brilliant idea!" said Lady Amelia.

The older lady was so shocked that she stopped fanning herself. "Amelia, you can't agree to this dreadful plan! You and this little scrap of a girl, laying a trap for a murderous highwayman? What nonsense, she's far too young! Oh, I think I'm going to faint . . ." She swayed, her eyes half closed, but she stood up straight again when it was obvious that no one was going to run over and catch her.

"She loves making a fuss, doesn't she?" Jewel muttered to Sophie. Sophie had to swallow a giggle.

"You simply can't, Amelia, I won't allow it." The older lady shut her fan with a *snap*.

"But, Cousin Flora, we must!" Lady Amelia insisted. "How would you feel if one of your friends was held up by that rogue? And imagine how exciting it will be to tell everyone! You will be a heroine!" She winked at Sophie.

"Oh, do you really think so?" gasped Cousin Flora.

"Of course!" said Mr Joy.

"We must go and get ready," said Lady Amelia. She led Cousin Flora away before she could change her mind.

Mr Joy rubbed his hands together. "Well done, Sophie! You stay here and I'll go and get my eldest boy, Billy. We'll need a strong lad to make sure we can hold Galloping Jim once we catch him."

He got back on to his horse and Sophie watched them trot out of the stable-yard. Jewel nudged her. "Come on, Sophie! You need to find something to wear so you look like a coachman."

Looking round the yard, Sophie spotted a big black coat with gold braid round the sleeves, and a three-cornered hat, hanging on a hook. "Do you think I could borrow those?" she asked.

Jewel nodded. "They must belong to the

injured coachman," he said. "I'm sure he won't mind."

Sophie put them on, rolling up the big sleeves and tipping the hat forward to hide her face. "What do you think?"

"Perfect," Jewel declared. "No one will know you're a girl!"

Sophie waited all afternoon at Grey Manor. The stable boy offered to share his lunch with her, but Sophie was too nervous to eat. Instead, she brushed Jewel until his coat shone like polished coal. The other carriage pony, Shadow, was exactly the same size and colour as Jewel.

When it started to get dark, Sophie and the stable boy harnessed the ponies to Lady Amelia's carriage. Jewel whispered instructions to Sophie so that she knew how to buckle the leather straps into place. Then they took the carriage round to the front of the house to wait for Lady Amelia and Cousin Flora.

When the two ladies appeared at the top of the steps, Sophie could see why they had needed all afternoon to get ready. Lady Amelia was wearing a magnificent blue dress embroidered with flowers made from tiny pearls and silver thread that twinkled as she moved. Her hair was swirled on her head so that it stood up like a tower, and ropes of pearls were woven through it to match the flowers on her dress. Two silver feathers were held in her hair by a diamond clasp. Sophie thought she looked like something out of a fairy tale!

"Good luck, Sophie!" Lady Amelia called before climbing into the coach. Cousin Flora followed her, tucking her rustling lilac skirt round her legs as she sat on the padded velvet seat.

Mr Joy and Billy ran up the drive just in time, looking rather red-faced and breathless. They clambered into the coach and crouched on the floor so that no one could see them. Sophie giggled when she heard

Cousin Flora grumbling about sharing a coach with the men. She stroked Jewel's mane, and Shadow's too, so he didn't feel left out. Feeling very proud, she climbed up to her seat and picked up the reins.

"Let's go!" Sophie slapped the reins lightly on the ponies' backs and the coach moved forward with a jerk. Sophie gasped with excitement as the wind tugged at her hair.

They were off to catch Galloping Jim!

8. Sophie Springs the Trap

Sophie loved driving Lady Amelia's carriage! Jewel was brilliant at calling instructions to her, telling her when to pull on the reins and when to send the ponies forward at a brisk canter.

Soon they reached the heath. Sophie spotted the tree where she had first seen Galloping Jim's poster and her heart began to beat faster. She knew the crossroads wasn't far ahead.

As they passed the tree with the poster, Jewel whinnied, "Slow down, Sophie! We're almost there!"

Sophie pulled on the reins and the ponies
slowed to a trot. Suddenly Galloping Jim
shot out in front of them on a tall black
horse. He stopped the horse so sharply that
it reared up, its front hoofs striking the air.
"Stand and deliver!" he shouted.

Sophie's heart leaped into her mouth. She
could tell Jewel was frightened too, because

his ears were pinned back and his tail swished.

Sophie felt the coach rock beneath her. Mr Joy and Billy were creeping out of the other door to grab Galloping Jim! She had to distract him so he didn't spot them. Jewel snorted loudly and scraped his hoof on the ground to cover the noise of the coach springs creaking. Sophie was very proud of him.

"Don't hurt us!" she shouted as gruffly as she could.

Galloping Jim threw back his head and roared with laughter. He dismounted and looped his horse's reins over a nearby branch. Then he approached the door of the coach. "Hand over your jewels!" he ordered.

Lady Amelia leaned out of the coach window. She gasped and covered her eyes as

Galloping Jim reached her. Sophie guessed she was distracting the highwayman's attention from Mr Joy and Billy as well. She was impressed that Lady Amelia was as brave as she was beautiful.

"Help! Robbers!" Cousin Flora shrieked.

Suddenly there was a scuffling noise, and Mr Joy and Billy dashed round the coach behind Galloping Jim. He let out a shout, but Mr Joy threw a sack over his head before he could run away. The highwayman kicked and struggled as Billy tied a rope around his arms. He was well and truly caught!

Sophie hopped down from the coachman's box and opened the coach door with a bow. "Lady Amelia, we have a guest for you!"

Mr Joy and Billy heaved Galloping Jim

on to the floor of the coach. He lay in a heap, wriggling and muttering.

Lady Amelia beamed. "Excellent! I've always thought this coach could do with a footstool. Don't you agree, Cousin Flora?"

"Oh yes," said Cousin Flora, looking much braver now Galloping Jim was tied up. And both ladies placed their dainty dancing shoes on the highwayman's back!

"That's a job well done," said Mr Joy, climbing into the coach. "Billy, you ride Galloping Jim's horse back to the forge. Sophie, let's get this villain under lock and key!"

Sophie pushed back her three-cornered hat and threw her arms round Jewel's neck. "You were so brave! And you were wonderful too, Shadow!"

She jumped back on to the coachman's box and clicked her tongue to send the ponies forward. They'd caught Galloping Jim! Lucy wouldn't have to live with her horrid uncle any more!

Lucy was waiting in the village square when they returned, wrapped in a warm cloak and holding a lantern. She looked amazed when she saw Sophie driving Lady Amelia's coach. When Mr Joy dragged out his struggling prisoner, she gasped. "Uncle Jim!"

"He tried to hold up the coach," Sophie explained. "I know you didn't want me to tell Mr Joy, but I had to!"

Lucy nodded sadly. "I know you did."

"Where will you go?" Sophie asked.

Lucy shrugged. "I don't know. I don't have any other relatives. Perhaps I'll have to go to the poorhouse."

Sophie wasn't sure what the poorhouse was, but it sounded horrible. Her heart sank. Had she and Jewel just made things worse for Lucy? Jewel blew softly in her ear and Sophie patted him, feeling tears prick in her eyes.

"Nonsense!" Mr Joy came back from locking Lucy's uncle in a shed at the back of his cottage. "You can move in with us, Lucy. Mrs Joy and I have always wanted a daughter."

Lucy's face lit up. "Really? Thank you so much!"

Sophie felt very pleased for her. Now Lucy would never be lonely again. And even better, she wouldn't have to rob any more coaches, or cook and clean for her uncle.

Lady Amelia leaned out of her carriage. "Congratulations, Sophie! You and your brave pony should be very proud of yourselves." She opened her little beaded purse. "Here, take this." She handed Sophie a shiny golden coin. "Well done, my dear."

Sophie blushed and stroked Jewel, who snorted and tossed his head. "I can feel the magic tugging us back to the carousel," he said.

"Quick, you need to unharness me." Sophie undid the straps and led him out from between the shafts of the carriage. His saddle was still at Grey Manor, so she climbed on bareback, leaning down to give Lucy one last hug goodbye.

"Will you come back one day?" Lucy called as she trotted away.

"I hope so!" Sophie called back. "Goodbye! Goodbye, everyone!"

She hung on tight as Jewel cantered out of the village. He didn't slow down even when the dark, shadowy woods loomed around them. Sophie smiled as she remembered how nervous he'd been at the start of their journey. As she reached down to give him a pat, the misty shadows seemed to draw closer and change colour.

Now Sophie and Jewel were galloping through a silvery pink cloud of sparkles. Sophie felt Jewel's gallop steady into a gentle rise and fall. The mist cleared and Sophie found she was gripping a twisty golden pole. Jewel's shining coat was black paint again and Sophie was sitting on a wooden saddle. She could see her parents and Molly waving to her as the Magic Pony Carousel slowed down. The adventure was over.

Sophie dismounted and went to stroke Jewel's nose one last time. The jewels in his browband seemed to wink at her. As she opened her fingers, she saw a glint of gold. It was Lady Amelia's golden coin!

Sophie clutched it tight and put her face close to Jewel's wooden ear. "I'll never forget you, ever!" she whispered happily.

Collect three tokens and get this funky Magic Pony Carousel photo frame!

There's a token at the back of each Magic Pony Carousel book – collect three tokens and you can get your very own, totally free Magic Pony Carousel photo frame!

Send your three tokens, along with your name, address and parent/guardian's signature (you must get your parent/guardian's signature to take part in this offer) to: Magic Pony Carousel Photo Frame Offer, Marketing Dept, Macmillan Children's Books, 20 New Wharf Road, London N1 9RR

Magic Pony Carousel
Photo Frame Offer

1 Token

Collect 3 tokens and get your free photo frame!
Valid until 31/12/06

Star

Poppy Shire

The carousel music grew louder and the horses swooped through the air as they gathered speed. The breeze blew on Laura's cheeks and the fairground lights seemed to glitter and twinkle around her. To her surprise the breeze felt warm, like on a summer's day, and the air began to glow and shimmer like summery mist. She looked up and gasped. It was no longer a cool autumn evening – instead the sky was a beautiful bright blue, with the sun blazing down. And she wasn't holding on to the golden pole any more. She had real leather reins in one hand and a rope lasso in the other!

Coming soon . . .

Poppy Shire

The carousel began to spin faster, and the fairground became a blur of laughing faces. Everything started to disappear in a rainbow mist. Emily blinked. She wanted to rub her eyes, but they were going so fast, she didn't dare let go of Crystal's reins. Silvery sparkles whirled around her, and the rainbow colours of the fairground changed to dazzling white. Everything shone and glittered with light, and Emily gasped out loud. This wasn't the fairground any more. She and Crystal were in the middle of a snowstorm!

Coming soon . . .

Poppy Shire

Chloe patted Flame's shiny wooden neck, then held on tight to the twisty golden pole. The carousel began to turn, lifting her gently up and down. Chloe pictured what it would be like to ride across the desert with the sun beating down. She could almost feel the warm rays on her skin . . . But then the air began to shimmer, and Chloe saw swirls of pink glitter falling around her. She rubbed her eyes. She must be imagining things! But no – the glitter was still falling softly.

"Ow!" she exclaimed as specks flew into her face. "What's that?"

Books coming in 2006

The prices shown below are correct at the time of going
to press. However, Macmillan Publishers reserves the right to
show new retail prices on covers, which may differ from those
previously advertised.

Magic Pony Carousel: Sparkle	0 330 44041 1	£3.99
Magic Pony Carousel: Brightheart	0 330 44042 X	£3.99
Magic Pony Carousel: Star	0 330 44043 8	£3.99
Magic Pony Carousel: Jewel	0 330 44044 6	£3.99
Magic Pony Carousel: Crystal	0 330 44597 9	£3.99
Magic Pony Carousel: Flame	0 330 44598 7	£3.99

All Pan Macmillan titles can be ordered from our website,
www.panmacmillan.com, or from your local bookshop and are
also available by post from:

Bookpost, PO Box 29, Douglas, Isle of Man IM99 1BQ
Credit cards accepted. For details:
Telephone: 01624 677237
Fax: 01624 670923
Email: bookshop@enterprise.net
www.bookpost.co.uk

Free postage and packing in the United Kingdom